The Santa Committee

An Interactive Christmas Adventure!

Written by
Tiffany Rhodes & McGhie Allan

First published in the United States in 2024.

For more information: www.santacommittee.com
First paperback edition October 2024 Tiffany Rhodes and McGhie Allan assert the moral right to be identified as the authors of this work.
Published by Elfanore, LLC

To James and Georgia, You two are the spark that ignited the magic of this Christmas story. Your wonder, joy, and love inspired us to create this tale. It's been our honor to adopt this Christmas tradition with you and watch you grow into joy spreaders, spreading love and kindness throughout the year. May this story remind you of the magic within you and the importance of sharing it with others. We love you more than words can express.

- Mom and Dad

Sugar Shadow
Enchanted
Forest
NORTH

Welcome, dear friend!

If you have stumbled upon this tale, it was meant for you, as it s a magical story that will change your holiday seasons forever. I am Elfanore, the once-retired Head Elfress of the Enchanted Sugar Shadow Forest, a mystical village located in the North Pole. After 250 years as Santa's right-hand elf, I never could have imagined the story I am about to tell you.

My home, the Enchanted Sugar Shadow Forest, is a wondrous place where the scent of freshly baked gingerbread fills the air, and the cheerful songs of my fellow elves echo through the trees. Despite my youthful appearance, I have spent a lifetime overseeing the creation of toys, candies, and desserts, infusing each with special elf magic.

Our workshop, perpetually blanketed in soft snow and twinkling colored lights, with gingerbread fixtures, is where innovative elves work alongside our leader, Santa Claus—a mystical figure who requires no introduction.

Merry Christmas!

As you are a curious young soul, I must dispel some common misconceptions about elves before beginning my tale. Firstly, our voices are not squeaky; we sound just like you, not like a squirrel. We have pointy ears but do not always wear pointy shoes, reserving them for special occasions like birthdays and Christmas. Additionally, we do not wear bells on our hats; imagine the ringing of hundreds of bells in one tiny workshop! You would never be able to hear our beautiful voices singing Christmas carols all day or the magical hooves of the Reindeer Express delivering this week's copy of "The Christmas Tree Times."

Lastly, the most egregious mistruth of all: we are not fairies. Let us simply say that they are our very, very distant cousins—who are more naughty than nice!

Our story begins just after I retired as Head Elfress and commenced a new, happy, and quiet life.

Late one evening, amidst the soft candlelight of my village home, I sat in my cozy armchair, surrounded by toys and half-finished crafts. An unexpected knock at the door sprung me to my feet, and with a snap of my fingers, I swung the door open to reveal Santa Claus himself.

was overjoyed by this surprise until I quickly noticed a hint of concern tempering his usual jolliness.
Elfanore, my old friend," Santa greeted me, "I need your help." His voice was low and serious.

I invited him to sit by the crackling fireplace and offered him a warm cup of gingerbread tea. With a tear caught on his cheek, he sat down.

"Elfanore, your talent for creating Christmas magic is unparalleled," Santa said. "I believe your skills are precisely what we need to address a pressing issue. The world's joy levels have plummeted, and it's not just about children believing in me. It's about spreading Christmas joy to everyone, regardless of age or belief. People are no longer spreading joy as they once did. Without this Christmas joy, I fear we might need to scale back Christmas or, worse, cancel it altogether." Santa buried his hands in his lap.

Listening to Santa's words ignited an unfamiliar surge of worry within me. Undoubtedly, every great problem has a great solution, and I was determined to find one.

"Tell me more, Santa," I asked eagerly.

"Well, Elfanore," Santa continued, "we need to make something special—a creation that embodies the essence of Christmas joy. Something that will warm hearts, spark wonder, and remind people of the season's magic."

I paced the room, thinking, scribbling idea after idea onto sheets of paper, crumpling and tossing the imperfect ones into the crackling fireplace until genius struck.

"I've got it!" I declared enthusiastically. "It's not a something; it's not a toy or a candy-topped dessert. No, this solution is bigger than all of that! We will create the first-ever Santa Committee!"

"We'll enlist children from around the globe and assign them wondrous tasks to spread joy, starting in their homes, neighborhoods, and schools."

"Brilliant!" Santa exclaimed, his eyes sparkling with renewed cheer. "With your elf-magic expertise and the children's boundless imagination, we'll bring smiles far and wide. Together, we'll remind the world of Christmas joy's true meaning!"

We discussed our plan throughout the night over several cups of gingerbread tea. As the holidays approached, we searched for the first recruit. Santa and I watched through a magical mirror, witnessing scenes from past Christmases. Among millions of exceptional candidates, we found an ideal candidate: Ann, a bright-eyed young girl with joy illuminating her face as she raced through snow-covered streets, leaving footprints of unlimited energy.

With a flick of my wrist, the magical mirror revealed Ann's focus on her simple Christmas traditions. Her small hands, once busy with play, now worked feverishly to decorate her home with twinkling lights and garlands, transforming her surroundings into a festive wonderland.

LETTERS
TO
SANTA

The next steps were clear: I would travel beyond the North Pole and secretly communicate with our first potential Santa Committee member. This twisted my stomach into a cinnamon roll of excitement.

I snapped my fingers, whispered my magic, and zoomed into a small town where Ann and her family resided. Upon arrival, I carefully laid my magical ladder against the house outside Ann's bedroom window

A storm raged outside, with rain pounding against her windowpane and thunder booming in the distance. Ann snuggled deeper into her bed, but flashes of lightning made her shiver. Seeking comfort, she dashed down the hallway to her parents' room, only to find them fast asleep.

I snapped my fingers again, and a candy cane materialized in her room. With a wave of my hand, I guided it to the foot of her bed. From the shadows, I watched as she returned to her room and discovered the candy cane, her eyes sparkling with wonder

I sensed her curiosity and knew my plan was working. With another wave, I filled the room with soft Christmas music and the scent of freshly baked cookies—a tricky spell, but worth it to see her smile.

Once she was asleep, I made my move. Quiet as a mouse, I tiptoed into her room and placed a note at the foot of her bed, ensuring she would see it first thing in the morning.

"Urgent! Santa Needs Your Help!" the note read. "Christmas joy is running low, and Santa needs YOU to save the holiday." The note included an official application to join the Santa Committee and a series of questions to determine her eligibility to join this dedicated group of Christmas joy spreaders tasked with completing twenty-four Christmas tasks before Christmas morning.

As I finished, I took one last look at the sleeping girl. With a silent whoosh of my frosty magic, I disappeared into the night, leaving behind a trail of sparkling stardust that floated gently onto her pillow like a blessing.

When Ann awoke, she found the note and application and excitedly ran down the hall to find her Mother. "Mom, what makes Christmas magic happen?" Ann asked. Her mom smiled warmly, "It's the love and joy we share with others. When we give, help, and care for others, that's the Christmas Spirit. Why do you ask?"

LETTERS
TO

Well, last night, I could have sworn I heard Christmas music and smelled the most delicious smells, but I guessed I was dreaming until I found this note!" She shared the note and application with her mom.

Her mom asked, "Do you think you have what it takes to be selected to the Santa Committee?"

"Yes, of course!" Ann exclaimed. "I was born for this!"

Together, they gathered every crayon, pencil, marker, paint, and even glitter, spreading them across the kitchen table. Her mom joined in, helping her create an extraordinary application illustrating Ann's Christmas spirit and readiness to help. Ann cheerfully decorated the application with her own Christmas doodles.

With their masterpiece complete, Ann and her mom carefully placed the letter in an envelope, sealed it, and walked to the mailbox. Ann proudly dropped the letter inside, her eyes sparkling with excitement.

As they returned inside, a gentle breeze stirred, carrying a faint jingling sound—a sign that Ann's message had been heard.

Back at the North Pole, I presented Ann's application to Santa, who sat at his grand oak desk, a twinkle in his eye as he reviewed the documents.

"These are certainly interesting," he mused, his eyes lighting up with merriment. "Look at these little drawings—a Christmas tree and a jolly elf. How curious."

Taking the papers from Santa's hands, I examined the doodles more closely. That's when I noticed the striking resemblance between the drawing and my attire: red boots, vibrant leggings, and a striped sweater—the very outfit I wore at that moment.

"Ann has doodled me!" I exclaimed.

TO

A wave of panic washed over me as I realized the implications. Had Ann seen me? Was it a coincidence, or had I been spotted during my secret mission? My heart racing, I grappled with the possibility that my cover might have been blown.

I retraced my steps, thinking and rethinking every move, as I savored my favorite dessert, "Jingle Bell Bliss" – a delightful concoction of sugary snowflakes, merry marshmallows, and twinkling tart cherries. As the deliciousness took over, I realized my cover was not blown, and i was simply a magical Christmas connection that meant we were on the right track.

Relieved, I bid Santa good night and continued monitoring Ann's progress. The following days passed in a blur of anticipation and excitement for Ann as she regularly checked the mailbox for an answer from the North Pole.

I observed the young applicant as she went about her days with a newfound sense of purpose, helping her mother with chores, walking the neighbor's dog, and dedicating time to tidying her room. Her kindness left a trail of warmth and happiness wherever she went.

Her excitement was contagious, and I couldn't help but feel a sense of pride knowing she had been accepted into the Santa Committee. I could barely contain my excitement, knowing what would happen next.

The Santa
Committee

One afternoon, Ann and her mom were washing dishes, the warm water and gentle suds providing a soothing accompaniment to their quiet routine. However, Ann's mind began to wander.

Her gaze drifted toward the window, and she remembered – she hadn't checked the mailbox in ten whole minutes! She rushed outside, the metal creaking as she opened the mailbox. Inside, a sweet peppermint scent wafted out.

My eyes sparkled as I saw Ann's heart skip a beat upon seeing her name on the special paper. She opened it, and her face lit up.

"SAAAAAAAAANTA!" she screamed, her loudest, happiest scream ever. "It's Santa! I'm in! I'm an official Santa Committee member!"

Her mom beamed with pride. "You did it! You're a Santa Committee member!" Their neighbors poured out into the street, curious about the commotion.

One concerned neighbor shouted, "What's all the fuss about?" Ann exclaimed, "I'm helping Santa!"

I smiled, knowing this moment marked the beginning of Ann's extraordinary adventure as a Santa Committee member.

Every morning, Ann found a special note from me hidden in a surprise spot—perhaps on the breakfast table, tucked in a lunchbox, clipped to a backpack, or in an Advent calendar. On each note, a sprinkle of holiday cheer would burst forth, revealing the day's fun task to help spread the Christmas Spirit

The challenges were always a delightful surprise, and Ann eagerly anticipated each new adventure. One day, she might scatter sugary sweetness throughout the town, "candy-bombing" parks and playgrounds, leaving treats for children to discover. The next day, she crafted beautiful, handmade Christmas cards, spreading warmth and cheer to those in need

My tasks were designed to inspire creativity and kindness, bringing joy not just to Ann but to her whole neighborhood and those around her.

SUGAR

Application For the Santa Committee

Join the Magic!

We're looking for kind and joyful children to join the Santa Committee! If you're excited to spread Christmas cheer and help make the holiday season brighter, fill out this application:

Section 1: About You

1. Name:

2. Age:

3. What makes you special and unique?

Section 2: Christmas Spirit

1. What does Christmas mean to you?

2. How do you show kindness and kindness to others during the holiday season?

3. What's your favorite holiday tradition?

Section 3: Santa Committee Tasks

1. Would you be willing to complete daily tasks to spread joy and kindness? Yes No

2. How would you help spread Christmas magic in your community?

3. Can you keep secrets and work with Elfanore and Santa? Yes No

Section 4: Elf-sized Promise

I promise to:
Be kind and helpful to others
Keep the Christmas spirit alive
Follow Elfanore's guidance
Keep Santa's secrets

Signature: ______________________________

Good Luck!
Elfanore, Head Elfress of the Enchanted Sugar Shadow Forest

The Santa Committee Acceptance Letter

Dear:

Congratulations!

We are thrilled to inform you that you have been selected to join the prestigious Santa Committee, led by Elfanore, Head Elfress of the Enchanted Sugar Shadow Forest!

Your application shone brightly, showcasing your kind heart, Christmas spirit, and eagerness to spread joy. We believe you will make a valuable addition to our team.

As a Santa Committee member, you will:

- Receive daily tasks to spread Christmas joy
- Help keep the Christmas magic alive

Welcome to the Santa Committee!

Santa Claus

DAILY SANTA COMMITTEE TASK TO SPREAD JOY

CREATE A CHRISTMAS COUNTDOWN

CREATE HANDMADE SIGNS FOR THE FRONT WINDOWS THAT SAY "MERRY CHRISTMAS!"

MAKE CHRISTMAS ORNAMENTS

CREATE FANTASTIC CHRISTMAS CARDS FOR ALL OF YOUR FAMILY

CANDY-BOMB YOUR FAVORITE FRIENDS OR NEIGHBORS

MAKE CHRISTMAS CARDS FOR THE ELDERLY

BAKE AND DECORATE GINGERBREAD COOKIES

WATCH YOUR FAVORITE CHRISTMAS MOVIE

WRITE YOUR OWN CHRISTMAS STORY, DON'T FORGET TO INCLUDE ELFANORE

MAKE MERRY CHRISTMAS CALLS TO AS MANY PEOPLE AS YOU CAN

ROCK OUT TO CHRISTMAS MUSIC

MAKE HOT COCOA WITH A PEPPERMINT CA

WRITE DOWN A BIG CHRISTMAS WISH YOU HAVE FOR THE WORLD

BAKE A CHRISTMAS RECIPE

MAKE CHRISTMAS GIFTS OR GO CHRISTMA SHOPPING

HELP SOMEONE IN NEED

DECORATE YOUR ROOM WITH CHRISTMAS FLARE

WRITE A CHRISTMAS LETTER TO SANTA

WRITE A CHRISTMAS LETTER TO YOUR PARENTS

DONATE TO YOUR LOCAL FOOD BANK

DONATE PET SUPPLIES TO YOUR LOCAL SHELTER

"The Santa Committee Official Document"

GIFT TOYS TO A CHILDREN'S HOSPITAL

START A NEW FAMILY TRADITION

MAKE A BIG BATCH OF SPICED CIDER

SEE A LIGHT SHOW

HOST A CHRISTMAS COOKIE SWAP

HOST A CHRISTMAS CRAFT NIGHT

START A CHRISTMAS SINGALONG

NEIGHBORHOOD CAROLING

CUT PAPER SNOWFLAKES

DECORATE A GINGERBREAD HOUSE

SPEND TIME VOLUNTEERING

MAKE HOMEMADE CANDY

TAKE A FAMILY PHOTO

WRAP GIFTS

GO ICE SKATING

MAKE PLACE CARDS FOR CHRISTMAS DINNE

MAKE A CHRISTMAS PLAYLIST

DRESS UP YOUR PET FOR THE HOLIDAYS
SHOP AT A HOLIDAY MARKET

Printed in the USA
CPSIA information can be obtained
at www.ICGtesting.com
CBRC090828141124
17319CB00020B/278

* 9 7 9 8 2 1 8 5 2 6 6 9 6 *